ORDINARY AUDREY

With thanks to Annika Harris for all
your patience and support – D.R.

To Chris – P.H.

tiger tales
an imprint of ME Media LLC
202 Old Ridgefield Road, Wilton, CT 06897
First published in the United States 2001
Originally published in Great Britain 2001 by Gullane Children's Books, London
Text © 2001 Peter Harris   Illustrations © 2001 David Runert
First US Edition
Printed in Belgium
1 3 5 7 9 10 8 6 4 2

Library of Congress Cataloging-in-Publication Data

Harris, Peter, 1933–
   Ordinary Audrey / by Peter Harris ; illustrated by David Runert.— 1st U.S. ed.
      p. cm.
Summary: Outlaws are headed for town and Deadwood Deb is on vacation, but
her twin sister, five-year-old Ordinary Audrey, just might be able to outsmart them.
   ISBN 1-58925-014-1 (hardcover)
   [1. Robbers and outlaws—Fiction. 2. West (U.S.)—Fiction. 3. Tall
tales.] I. Runert, David, 1971– ill. II. Title.
   PZ7.H24347 Or 2001
   [E]—dc21
                                        2001000946

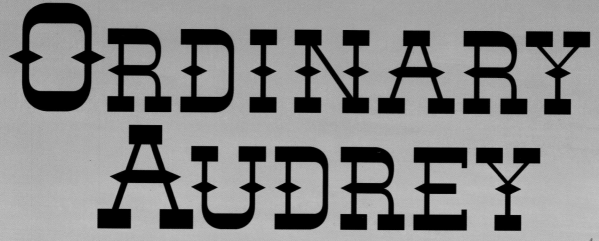

ORDINARY AUDREY

by **PETER HARRIS**

Illustrated by **DAVID RUNERT**

tiger tales

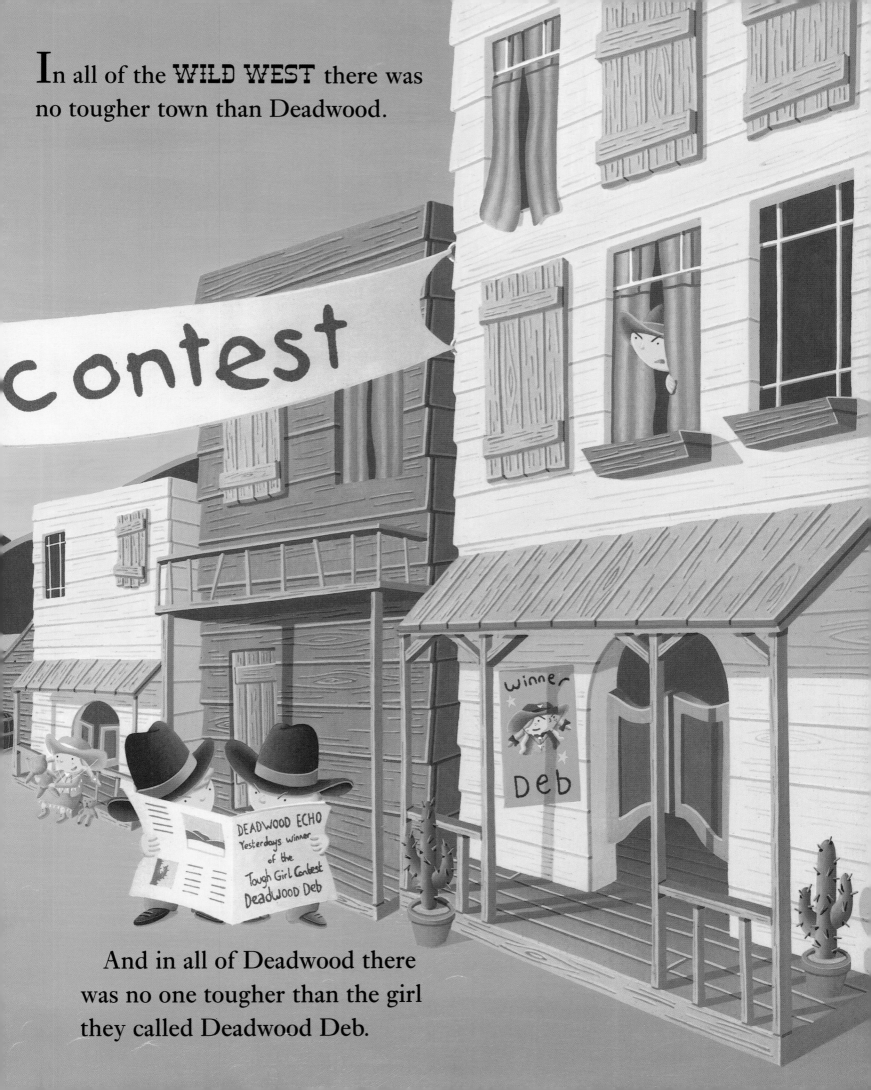

In all of the **WILD WEST** there was no tougher town than Deadwood.

And in all of Deadwood there was no one tougher than the girl they called Deadwood Deb.

Deb was so tough she could out-lasso...

out-snarl...

and out-eat even the toughest cowboy in the land.
Which isn't bad when you're only five years old.

So when news came that the meanest outlaws in the West were headed for Deadwood, "No problem!" the townsfolk said. "We'll make Deb our sheriff. She'll soon send 'em running."

"Nope, she won't," drawled Doc Wesley. "Deadwood Deb's on vacation down in Florida, wrestling alligators."

"Of course," he continued, "we could always make Deb's twin sister, Ordinary Audrey, our sheriff."

Now, Ordinary Audrey was very ordinary indeed.

She liked playing with teddy bears...

and swinging on swings— just as long as they didn't go too high.

When it came to being tough, though, she couldn't even out-lasso, out-snarl, or out-eat Doc Wesley's fat old tabby cat. But she *had* been known to out-sick the other kids after eating too much cake at parties.

So why choose Ordinary Audrey to be the sheriff?
"Because," said Doc Wesley. "She looks just like Deb, so if we dress her up like Deb too, those outlaws will take one look at her and scream, '**It's Deadwood Deb!**' then run for their lives!"

But why did Ordinary Audrey agree to be the sheriff?
Well, wearing that silver star made her feel very important . . .
and she did like the way it sparkled in the sun.

But on the day the outlaws rode into town,
Ordinary Audrey didn't feel important at all.
No, sir. She felt scared. Plumb scared.

"I'm D-D-Deadwood Deb," she stuttered. "I'm p-p-plenty tough," she went on, telling an even bigger lie. "So you'd b-b-better not start any t-t-trouble."

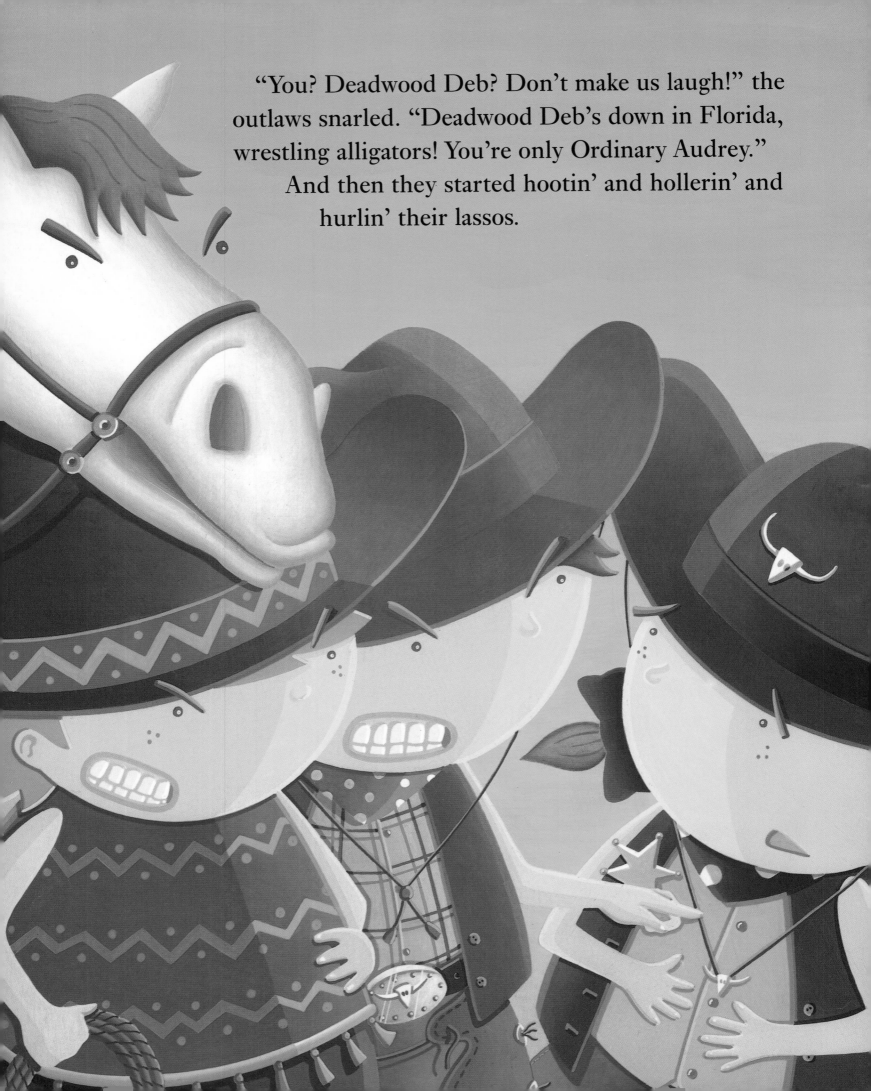

"You? Deadwood Deb? Don't make us laugh!" the outlaws snarled. "Deadwood Deb's down in Florida, wrestling alligators! You're only Ordinary Audrey." And then they started hootin' and hollerin' and hurlin' their lassos.

Now, Deadwood Deb would have stayed to fight. But not
Ordinary Audrey. She jumped on the nearest horse and rode
lickety-split out of there, with those outlaws laughing at her.
And she didn't stop riding until she reached Peaceful Springs.

Well, those springs may have been peaceful, but little Audrey sure wasn't. One of those varmints had busted her sheriff's badge! And you know how she felt about that silver star.

Then Audrey started thinking just what those mischief-makers might be up to in Deadwood . . . and she realized that the folks back home needed her help.

Now, Audrey knew she couldn't out-lasso or out-snarl those outlaws, but she was pretty sure she could out-smart them. So Ordinary Audrey thought up one peach of a plan.

"Please, Mr. Railroad Man, I need a ticket to Deadwood," said Audrey, as she walked into the station. "I'd like to send a telegram, and do you know any place that sells suitcases?"

Back in Deadwood, the outlaws were being as mean as coyotes in a cactus patch, when the telegram arrived with their names on it.

"Whoopee! It says here we've won the lottery!" they hooted. "$100,000 will be coming our way on the 6:18 train! Let's get down to the railroad depot!"

And that was just where Ordinary Audrey wanted them to be.

When the 6:18 train from Peaceful Springs rolled into Deadwood, Ordinary Audrey got off carrying the suitcase she'd bought. She pulled herself up straight, and twisted her mouth into a snarl—just like her sister's—

and she looked those outlaws right in the eye.

"Well if it isn't the cowardly rattlesnakes who ran my twin sister out of town!" she snarled, real mean. "BOYS, am I going to teach you a lesson!"

And did they say "Don't make us laugh!" like they had before? No, sir! They screamed,

"It's Deadwood Deb! The real one!"

And they left town even faster than Audrey had, and she'd been riding a horse!

The townsfolk couldn't believe their eyes. They crept out of their hiding places and came out to cheer.

"Well if that doesn't beat all!" the Deadwood folk said. "Just watch those varmints skedaddle!"

"You know, we should put up a statue of our Ordinary Audrey," said Doc Wesley. "And while we're at it, we'll give her a new name too!"

And that is exactly what they did. From that day to this, that brave little girl has been known as
Extraordinary Audrey.